SCARLETT HART
MONSTER HUNTER

Marcus Sedgwick   Thomas Taylor

SCARLETT HART
MONSTER HUNTER

:01
First Second
New York

For MG
—M.S.

For Max and Benjy
—T.T.

RRRRRRMM..

RRRRRRRRR

Midnight...

EEEEEEEEEE

The Academy has announced that another monster is on the loose.

RRRRRRRRRRRRRRRRRRRRR

I really think you ought to put your seat belt on, Miss Hart.

CLATTER
CLUNK

There you are!

The thing has struck twice by the White Whale Warehouse.

Park up, Napoleon, and we'll have a nose around.

Very good, miss.

It'll be more "killing" than "capturing," then?

Yes, I think we'll go for the "fizzer."

Did you put new film in the camera, miss?

Of course!

We really need this one, Napoleon.

I'm aware of our impecuniosity. However, I think we should exercise caution.

The bounty's 150 crowns!

Same old Napoleon White. Always worrying!

Anyway, I've got a plan.

It's very simple. We wait till the monster appears, I throw the bomb, it blows up, you take the photos. Then we put our feet up.

Leaping lizards!

PUFF
ZZZZ

SSSS... ...TIK!

BOOM

POUF

Better luck next time, Hart!

NOM!

SSS...

Ha ha ha!

Hey! You're Scarlett Hart! The great monster hunter!

Me? Never heard of her. I'm just a great idiot.

The way you saved me! That was...

HONK

ONK HONK

Time we left, miss! The Watch are coming!

The Watch?

Thank you!

BOING!

I do wish you'd mind your feet on the seats, miss.

Oi! You!

SCREEEEEEEEECH

Stop!
COF!

Oh, gaskets and cylinder rings!

Miss?

We stink.

If I may, miss, I think the Count is the one who stinks.

Well...?

The Count!

15

...

Miss...

...about the camera...

It's okay.

We can buy another one.

Not just at the moment, miss.

Is it that bad?

Then we'll just have to capture the next monster, won't we? And then you can march it into the Academy and claim the big fat reward.

Yes?

Yes. That's just what we'll do.

Great! And now I'm going to bed.

My parents' room...

The next day, at the Royal Academy for the
Pursuit and Eradication of Zoological Eccentricities...

Known for ease
as *T.R.A.P.E.Z.E.*
or the Academy.

...?

RUMRUM RU

RRRUUMM

Screech!

You!

Here again, Hart? Why don't you just give up? I'd have thought you'd have learned your lesson by now. You're a terrible hunter.

I don't know what you're talking about.

Just wait until the Watch catch up with you.

Heh heh.

I, *er*, really do not know what you are talking about.

Underage monster hunting! That's what! And having your father's dusty old butler report your kills.

Yeh!

Napoleon isn't old.

I'd report you myself if I could get a nice photograph of you in action.

You...you wouldn't!

But then, you're so useless, I'd probably never get the chance.

Heh! Yeh.

Useless!

Just like your parents, no?

How dare you!

That's how they got themselves killed, isn't it?

You! You jumped-up *mustache waxer!* You're not even a *real count!*

Pea-brained tire muncher!

Scabby nosed cat eater!

SMAK

Animal-faced sewer dweller!

...

Put me down! Napoleon! Dog-bottomed ferret face!

That's somewhat uncalled for, miss.

Sorry, Napoleon. Not you...

Weasel-headed monkey brain!

VRRMM

Really, your skill with insults nearly rivals your father's...

Thank you.

*!#

VRMM

"The Black Dog of Suffolk County. Also known as Black Shuck. Ghost-dog with glowing red eyes. Has caused four deaths this past month alone. Last sighted in Devil's Hollow."

Oh, how nice.

"Beware! Once you have seen the glowing red eyes, your own death is inevitable."

They do like to make those things as lurid as possible, don't they?

We have to capture it, Napoleon. How are we going to do that if it's really a ghost?

More likely a village superstition. Someone's puppy got out of hand.

The reward's only twenty crowns, it can't be that fearsome.

Excuse me, miss, but we've arrived.

Good news, boys! Good news.

BANG

These people are from the city. They're monster hunters! They've come to kill Shuck!

HA HA HA HA
HA HA HA HA
HA HA

Come on, Napoleon. It smells in here, anyway.

Heh Heh Heh
Heh Heh
Ha!

Very good, miss.

Hey!

You want Shuck?

You've got ears, haven't you?

Only, I knows where 'e is. See?

31

So, Billy. You've seen Shuck?

'E comes out of there.

At midnight.

Whose place is this?

Old Westley Waterless.

Doesn't he know?

Westley don't know nothing. 'E's dead six years.

ZZz

Nearly midnight, miss.

ZZZ

KUK

Come on.

Whatcha g-gonna do?

This is for if he's real.

And this is for if he's not.

HOLY WATER

I can't hear a thing—

He's real enough!

Quick!

Miss! Wait!

VRRR RR

She always do that?

Rather a lot of her mother in her.

I do hope she's careful.

With Dorothy, I mean.

Look!

That where 'e come from?

FIGHT! The Black Dog of Suffolk County!

BLAM

Got you!

RRRRRRRR

Oh, gaskets...

Oh no! Napoleon!

SCREEEECH

Them eyes!
We're doomed!

Nice doggie.
Doggie want
a drinkie?

POP

Oh!

Really, miss. I do wish you'd take more care with Dorothy. She's a priceless heirloom.

Here. It's all we've got.

Do you think they'll pay out on the dog, Napoleon?

We have the majority of the beast in the bag. I think we'll be fine.

Morning...

Breakfast, my dear.

What...what time is it?

Half past eleven.

It can't be! I was going with Napoleon to claim the reward.

Now, you just rest. He's gone by himself. He'll be back soon.

I hate it when he does that.

It's not as if you can go inside anyway, is it, love?

40

I know, but—

In a couple of years you'll be old enough.

In a couple of years I could be dead.

CRUNCH

Miss! Don't say that. Some monster hunters go on for years.

It's not that dangerous, if you're careful.

Isn't that what my mother said to my father...?

Good as new. The old fusspot should be happy enough with that.

The old fusspot heard that.

Do neither of you understand the heritage of this car? The history?

One of only eleven Machen Roadsters ever made–

Ting Ting

EEEE

EECH

–and this one unique, thanks to the additional work by your father, miss.

Yes, Napoleon. We know. But we need Dorothy to work, don't we? Not sit in a museum.

Talking of work... twenty crowns!

Housekeeping money.

Good morning, Miss Hart. How are you? That scratch bothering you?

Hardly. That was one big mutt, wasn't it?

Indeed, miss. Fancy something a little closer to home?

MUMMY

43

A street in Theatre Land

You're very quiet, miss.

Do you know what day it is today?

Ah. Yes. I didn't know if I should...

Four years ago today. I can't believe it's been so long already.

How did it happen, Napoleon?

We've discussed this a number of times, miss.

SCREEEEECH!

I know. But they were good hunters.

The best. But even the best...

Stupid city! Stupid laws!

RRRRRR

I'm not allowed to hunt, but there's nothing to say I can't drive a car. Which is probably more dangerous.

It is, the way you drive, miss.

EEEEE

Hey, Napoleon, I meant to ask: If you left Dorothy with Mrs. White...

RRRRRAN

...how did you get the remains of the dog to the Academy?

Very carefully.

...

You know, there is one thing.

About your parents.

The day before they... Well, the day before, your father told me about something else.

He did?

You know they say there was a time when monsters didn't roam free?

I've heard that, yes.

Your father told me there is an ancient book that explains it all. Why the monsters came.

A book? What's it called?

The *Codex Monstrorum.*

But what does that have to do with my parents' death?

Rattle Rattle

I have absolutely no idea, miss. I'm sorry.

Side entrance?

Zzz

STAGE

47

This way...

!

Oh, look, miss.

Props!

Heh.

Hah! Napoleon!

Grab!

Aaah!

Hey, I'm only joking.

That dummy!

UUUUUUUUUR...

That's no dummy. That's the mummy!

Urrrr. Brains. Fresh brains...

UUUUURRRRR

Run!

!

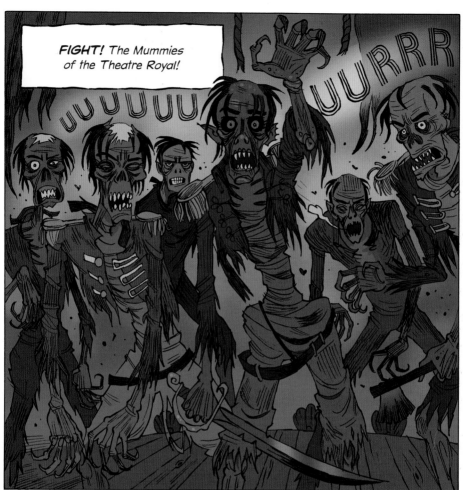

FIGHT! The Mummies of the Theatre Royal!

UUUUUU

UUURRR

BWAINS

Pistons and pumps! We're trapped.

THOCK

THAK!

It's curtains for you lot!

THUNK!!

UUUUUUUURRr...

AAAAAAGH...

UUUUUUURrr...

AAAAAGH!

Soon...

Nice idea, miss.

VRUM VRUM

AAAARG

BWAINS?

uuur...

VRRRRRRM

uuuur...

uuur...

uuuuuu...

Stop at the Salty Dog, miss. I'll take these beauties on to the Academy from there.

I'll be as fast as I can, miss.

I wish I could come with you.

One day, miss.

Napoleon. That book you told me about...?

The **Codex**, miss? Your father believed it explained everything about monsters.

Their effect on the world. The Tentacles of Terror, he called it.

T-tentacles?

It's a metaphor, miss. Your father used it to mean the fear that monsters make us live under.

EEEEEEE

A triple whisky and easy on the ice.

TAP TAP

Now, Scarlett, you know—

Just kidding. Ginger beer, please.

Right you are.

Waiting for Napoleon?

Yes. But shush.

Everyone's your friend here, Scarlett.

I know. But the Count's trying to get me in trouble.

The Count?

That phony!

To John and
Violet Hart.

Yeah. Sorry,
Scarlett.

Aye.

Hrum-um-us.

Thanks,
boys.

How's
business,
Scarlett?

Better. But that
toad-faced Count stole
our kill the other day.

Stankovic!
He should know
better than to
break the code.

Never
steal another
man's meat.

Or
woman's.

He's crossed
us once or twice,
hasn't he, boys?

Rhum-as-
hrum-rhum.

Quite! You know, I reckon his own mother would cross the street to avoid him.

He cost us 150 crowns. And we lost our camera, too.

That's bad. But you'd better take it slow for a while. Keep out of trouble. If Stankovic is gunning for you...

I know. But without a camera, we have to take everything in. Dead or alive.

Or un-dead, in this case.

Eight mummified soldiers, at twenty-five crowns apiece!

200 crowns!

FRRRP!

The ninny at the pay desk asked if we could make it fully-dead next time. I think we gave them quite a fright down at the Academy.

A street in Mulbery, the city

Ooh, look, Napoleon!

Can we?

We can.

But what will Mrs. White say?

Necessary business expenditure. Vital to the job.

Well? I'm about to close.

How delightful for you. In the meanwhile, perhaps you can sell us a camera.

That one!

That one? That one is very expensive. Perhaps something... cheaper.

That one!

It would help if I knew what it is for. What kind of use it will be put to.

...

It's for—

—holiday snaps.

Holiday snaps? It's a little—

It's perfect! We'll take it.

Later, back at Ravenwood Hall...

...

Ah! The young lady in question.

May I inquire as to your business here?

Inquire away. This person is summoned to the Academy. Tomorrow morning. On suspicion of underage monster hunting. Good evening.

Morning...

Miss Hart? It wouldn't help our cause to be late.

Is that where the notices come from?

Indeed. Miss, we should hurry.

Scarlett?

DEPT of IRREGULARITIES

TOC
TOC

Insofar as the above named person has been intimated to be pursuant of zoological eccentricities in full cognizance of the breach of articles 137 and 354 of City Regulations, 84th draft, the above named person is heretofore made aware that any subsequent misdemeanors by herself shall be subject to penal retribution as stipulated in sections 63 through 67 of the sentencing manual, 34th draft, namely that the goods, financials, and physical domesticity of the said person shall be confiscated forthwith!

Tak Tik Tak...

I beg your pardon?

I think you've been let off with a warning.

I have? Oh good!

But if they catch us again, they'll take Ravenwood away from us.

What? **They can't! You can't!** Hey, you! You **wouldn't dare!** Just you—

Time to go, I think. Thank you, your wordiness.

How did they know? Who told them?

Heh heh heh....

I think we may know that already.

Slurp

Here's to you, Count.

The Count!

CHIEF'S OFFICE

...!

BUMP

Miss Hart!

CLUNK
whirrr...

?

PING!

PLUCK!

...

...

GLUG GLUG
GLUG...

SPLOOSH

Mrs. White used to bring you here when you were little.

I remember.

We have to consider Ravenwood Hall, miss.

Don't say it!

We have to consider you.

I can take care of myself.

Not according to the law, miss. If you get caught, we will lose everything. Mrs. White and I will do our best for you, but we'll have to start again with nothing.

Is there a Plan B?

Yes. Sell the Hall now, while we have the chance. Right now, all we have is 175 crowns. And the Hall. Sell it and we can buy a little cottage somewhere and live off the proceeds of the sale...

Sell Ravenwood or have it taken from us? Some choice!

plop

There is another option, Napoleon.

There is?

Plan C. We keep hunting, and don't get caught.

Miss, I–

What do you think my father would have done? Or my mother?

I was afraid you'd say that...

Well?

Ghostly bishop on the rampage. 150 crowns. Scarlett, are you sure?

That night, in the Tyborne District...

tweak tweak

Napoleon, what are you doing?

I found these in your father's workshop. He called them ghost goggles.

Ghost goggles?

You're supposed to be able to see spooks through them.

But ghosts are visible anyway.

Not all the time. They only materialize when they want to *scare* you. With these, you can see them all the time.

Do they work?

I'm not sure. *Ah!* Here's the place.

75

THE NOBLE PIG

According to the notice, they've had to close down. Thanks to the bishop on the loose.

Standard ghost hunting kit, Napoleon.

FLOUR

That too, miss?

Just in case...

The trouble with ghost hunting is you have to do it at night.

Scared, miss?

Of course not!

Nor I.

Whirrr....

All clear.

Let's try upstairs.

These two ought to cover most eventualities.

THUMP

A-ha!

Reveal yourself, you beastly bishop!

"Beastly bishop"?

Sorry, miss. It just came out.

Now what?

whrrrr...

Hmm.
Nothing.

...

Napoleon?

Yes?

These goggles?

Yes?

They may not be necessary.

81

I'd call you a has-been, Hart, but you're more of a never-was.

Yeh!

Stinkovic! You rotten—

Too bad. Looked like you almost had that one. Leakey, why don't you take a picture of our friends for the nice folks down at the Academy?

You wouldn't!

He would.

Of course I would. Do it, Leakey.

Yeh!

Touch that camera again and I'll blast you and it to kingdom come!

We stink.

He stinks. There's something fishy about this.

You're right, Napoleon! And I know what it is.

Miss?

I broke the Kill-or-Capture Notice machine, yes? So how did he know about the bishop?

You're right!

Napoleon! Let's follow him.

CLik

ZZZZ...

ZZZ   Z...

What is this place?

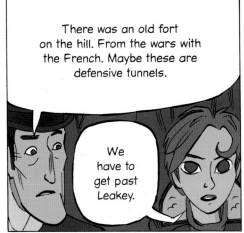

There was an old fort on the hill. From the wars with the French. Maybe these are defensive tunnels.

We have to get past Leakey.

I'll make a distraction, miss. Perhaps we can draw him away.

Shh! It's stinky pants!

One tug means lower, two means stop. Any more than that means pull me up like crazy.

Careful is my middle name.

Do be careful, miss, won't you?

Jemima is your middle name.

Don't remind me...

There! It's done. Be at the cathedral in half an hour to see what we have wrought.

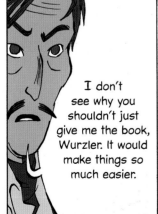

I don't see why you shouldn't just give me the book, Wurzler. It would make things so much easier.

How stupid do you think I am, Stankovic?

You know, I could just take it from you.

91

You little wretch!

You wouldn't dare!

One word from me and you'll be sent back to the gutter you came from!

Just stick to the bargain, Stankovic. And be at the cathedral.

CRASH!

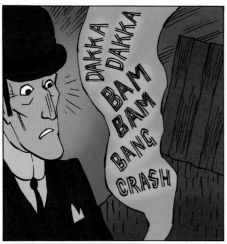

DAKKA DAKKA BAM BAM BANG CRASH

Miss! Miss Hart!

ZZZZIIIIP ZZZIIIP ZZZIIIP

Come out, come out wherever you are...

CLAK

Come out, come out wherever you are...

DACKA- DAK DACKA

Heh Heh Heh

?

BAM

POP

In you go...

DA KA D

CRAK

Guh! Urr!

GET THEM OFF!

Time to go, I think, Napoleon.

Very good, miss.

A street in the Royal Quarter.

Hello, little chap. *Hee hee.*

What is it, miss?

Can you believe that Stankovic is scared of spiders?

He's not the only one...

Hey, Napoleon! The Count! He was talking to another man.

Who?

Not sure. Bratwurst or something. But he had the *Codex*! He said, "It's done," and told Stankovic to head for the cathedral.

What's done?

I don't know, but I know where we're going now.

The cathedral precincts, miss?

Napoleon, you're number one!

?!

SCREEEEEEECH

Aiiii

FFFFFFFF

SSSSSSSS

EEEEEEEEE

Er...

Napoleon! Look!

We have to help them!

We do?

Go!

Er, yeh.

Are you okay?

POUF

CLIK

You...!

Miss! Look!

That Count!

We saved his miserable skin, and not so much as a thank you.

Never mind that, Napoleon. We know he's a complete cad. But we know something else now, too.

Namely?

The **Codex**. It doesn't just **explain** monsters. It can **summon** them! That's how Stankovic knew to come to the cathedral! They're **making** monsters!

Why?

For the bounty. Stankovic gets there first, makes the kill, takes the money.

And he splits it with the owner of the book, no doubt.

Exactly. Napoleon, we have to report this...

Miss, would you mind driving? I'm a little spent.

Oh!

Dorothy!

At least it's not my fault this time.

The Watch House

108

We want to speak to whoever's in charge.

RING RING...

You speak to me, and I decide if you speak to the captain.

RING

But we have to! We have a terrible crime to report.

The young lady is right. We have reason to believe that Count Stankovic is bringing monsters to life!

He's a monster hunter, why would he do that?

That's the point! He–

Stop wasting my time! Bringing monsters to life...? If you don't–

Sergeant!

MUCH later...

We stink.

Something does, but I don't think it's us. Not yet.

It's probably me.

Jack! What are you doing here?

Some watchmen arrested me! Said I was drunk!

So why do you smell so bad?

There was a disagreement...

...as a result of which I fell in a crate of fish.

But they got nothing on me. They'll have to let me out by six.

They've got **plenty** on us. Napoleon! They'll take Ravenwood away. That Count!

What's he got to do with it?

He took a photograph of us killing some gargoyles. Right after we'd saved his life!

The swine!

I saw him talking to a mysterious man. They have the **Codex**. They're using it to make monsters.

Make monsters? No, the **Codex**—

That's what I thought, but—

It's true! They're bringing monsters to life.

And the Count's taking the kills. The **Codex** is way more powerful than we thought. The Tentacles of Terror will spread wider and wider.

If only John and Violet were here...We need them now.

Oh, I'm sorry, Scarlett.

It's okay.

I wish they were here, too. They'd know what to do.

But they got themselves killed, didn't they?

Still, I don't regret who they were.

Well said, miss. If I may say so.

You may. What other kid could fence at the age of six or got flying lessons for her twelfth birthday?

That's the spirit, Scarlett.

That stinky Stankovic! This is all his fault! Why does he hate us so much?!

CREEEEEEEEEEE....

JANGLE

Jack Petit? Six o'clock. You are free to go.

...a very long time ago, when you were only a dream that was yet to be had by your parents.

It was the debutante's ball.

The first great social occasion for the young people of the city. Your father had been trying to find the courage to ask your mother to be his date.

Dad? Nervous? Never!

Don't you believe it. He was smitten by your mother the first time he saw her. But finally he asked her, and she said yes.

The trouble was, Stankovic had already asked your mother to go with him.

Stankovic? **Ugh, no!**

I'm afraid so. At the ball, there was a terrible scene. Stankovic called your mother something awful.

You said you'd go with **me**!

I said I'd *think* about it!

You little %*&%^@!

That's going too far, *Stinky-snitch*!

He called him stinky, too?

He did. Stop interrupting, you're making this very hard. Anyway, Stankovic went to punch your father...

...but he dodged, and...

...Stankovic fell over a balcony into a fountain.

He was humiliated. Everyone laughed at him. He left in a huff, and no one saw him for months.

When he came back, he was calling himself "count," and from then on, he had it in for your parents.

And now he
has it in for you...

Later...

What time is it, Napoleon?

Around four in the morning.

Can't sleep?

You know, if it's true about what the Count is up to... It's very dangerous. He doesn't know what he's doing. He could do anything.

He could **summon** anything. Napoleon, you're right. We have to stop him.

And whomever he's working with. But first we have to get out of here.

Oh, yes. I'd forgotten.

Don't worry, miss. While you were asleep I took the liberty of arranging an escape plan.

You did?

I did. Catcher Jack returned to the window, just here. I gave him the keys to Dorothy and instructions for Mrs. White.

You did?

I did. I only hope he's a careful driver—

BAM

Well, don't just stand there gawping!

Hurry!

Where are we going? Home?

The cathedral. Monsters on the loose!

119

But we killed all the gargoyles!

So you did. It's the rest of them that are causing trouble now.

?!

Everything in the cathedral is coming to life. And...*Oh!*

Jack!

BATTLE! *The Creepy Creatures of the Cathedral!*

Miss Hart!

She knows what she's doing, worry-boots!

And we have problems of our own.

Thanks!

AAAAAAAAAARGH....

That came from inside!

Easy...

Be nice to me.

125

You!

131

Napoleon! Go!

Miss?

Just go!

KSSSSSSS

No!

We can't fight that, Scarlett!

VRUUUM!

THWUMP!

SHIFT.

Get us home,
girl. If you can.

Tentacles, Napoleon! Tentacles!

I thought you said it was a *metaphor*!

We stink.

Ravenwood Hall

They can't really take it away from us, can they?

I'm afraid they can.

Meanwhile, that thing is on the loose! If only we weren't so stinky.

Agreed, miss.

The only thing that stinks around here is your attitudes!

Do you think your parents defeated the *White Phantom* or the *Vampire Queen of English Marsh* by sitting around complaining?

No, but—

No! So we're not going to, either.

But you saw the size of that thing!

True...

Mr. White, I wonder whether it's time we told Scarlett about the project...

The project?

The project?

Are you sure, Mrs. White?

Scarlett, your father was working on something before he died.

He was always working—

This was something different.

Something...big. I think you should come and see.

Have you been in here since...?

No.

There's something here you never saw...

CLICK

BRMBMBL... BRMBMBL...

Gaskets!

From the time of the French wars...

This is the only way...

...to a secret section of the attic...

139

Your father spent hours up here. **Days.**

Some project...

He would tell you he was away, but I'd bring him meals up here.

Does...does it have a name?

He was waiting until he finished it.

But it looks finished.

It requires an engine. A very *expensive* engine...

What kind?

The kind your father thought was the best in the world...

Only eleven were ever made...

...the engine of a Machen Roadster.

Dorothy!

But...but we can't!

Nothing else will defeat that monster. You know it.

Put Dorothy's engine in the plane...?

We'd only be borrowing it. And right now, poor Dorothy's not fit for anything.

Very well.

SMak!

Napoleon, you're wonderful! Let's get on with it.

Hey! There's just one thing. How do we get this thing out of here?

Voilà!

WZZ WZZZZ

And so...

TAK TAK TAK

FAZAZA...

munch...

TWEAK!

PHUT...

PHUT...

SPUTTER COF...

BANG!

ROAR

You're sure you can do this?

The controls are just like the plane I learned on. Well, mostly. I don't know what this one—

Don't touch that!

Why? What does it do?

I have no idea, but this thing is full of weaponry.

All set?

You bet, Mrs. White! That thing's probably eaten half the city by now.

KLIP KLIP

PHUT-PHUT-**PHOOM!**

Plenty of throttle, miss, if I may suggest?

Napoleon, stop worrying. I'll be fine!

See you...

CRANK!

...SOOOO...

VROOOOOR

149

Heh heh.
No problem.

What's this?

I must be seeing things...

!

What in Heaven's name did Stankovic do...?

...And where's the beast now?

Oh!

153

Let's see what Dad put in this thing...

KLIP KLIP KLIP...

MACHINE GUNS

Ah!

CLICK!

SHLAK!

SHOWDOWN!
The Tentacled Terror!

BLATTER BLATTER BLATTER

Missed me!

My turn...

BLATTER
SPATTER

156

159

Gaskets! That thing is tough.

And it's nearly reached the palace!

Oh, come on! There must be something that can at least tickle it!

KLIP
KLIP
KLIP
KL

KNOCKOUT GAS

BOUNCING BOMB

DEPTH CHARGE

LAST RESORT

Last resort?

Well, if it's my last resort...

...I'd better get in close...

...and make it...

KLAK

KLAK

CRASH

KZZZZZZZZZZZZZZzzzzzzzzzz

I stink.

Stankovic!

And **Bratwurst**! Or whatever your name is!

Take her away, immediately.

Yes, Chief Wurzler.

But he's in league with Stankovic. They've been making monsters!

I'd watch your tongue if I were you, Hart! **Take her!**

Y-Your...Your Royal Nobleness...

Stop blithering. Why are you treating this girl in this unseemly fashion?

She's a wanted criminal, Your Highness.

Nonsense! Anyone can see this girl has just saved the city. Not to mention the royal personage. Whatever crimes she has committed are of no further concern.

B-but, Your Majesty...

Do we make ourselves clear? We should be thanking her, not treating her like a hoodlum! Young lady, what is your name?

Scarlett Hart, Your Highness. And that man is responsible for—

Hart? That name seems familiar to us...

Perhaps you've heard of my parents. But that man, Your Wealthiness! He's been—

Hart? Yes, we recall. Hart, you are hereby thanked. And pardoned. Good evening to you.

But—!

Be quiet!

Let her speak. What is it, child?

We—I mean, that is, Napoleon White and I— we have reason to believe that Count Stankovic is responsible for this outbreak of monstrosities. That he and the chief are using an ancient book to bring monsters to life.

Really? Who are these men you speak of?

They're right...

...oh...

They were both there! Just now. I—

It sounds like a matter for the Watch. We suggest you speak to them.

We grow weary. Good night to you.

But—

But—

Never mind him. The main thing is that you're safe. And so is Ravenwood.

The Count...

But he's guilty! And Napoleon, if the chief of the Academy is guilty, too...

I know. We will have to tread very carefully, pardon from the prince or no.

Let's go home. Since you will arrive first, perhaps you could ask Mrs. White to pour me a glass of beer? A large one.

TING

PHUT PHUM...
PHOOM

KLAK

177

I'll follow the coast road home.

Napoleon!

Time to die, butler boy.

No!

PHUT...

KKKKKKRRK

Napoleon!

?!

I strongly suggest you reach for my hand.

Never! I don't need–!

SNAP

189

I hated him, but what a way to go...

You know who I feel sorry for?

Who?

The poor shark. Just think of the indigestion.

Napoleon! That's a terrible thing to say.

But what about Chief Wurzler? *He* knows that *we* know! We need to do something!

Maybe, but not today. It's time we went home. Mrs. White will be worrying herself silly.

No, Napoleon. You're the White who worries.

Well, really, Miss Hart.

Fin

Heroes

Scarlett concepts

Napoleon concepts

Monsters

Zombie Soldiers

Zombie designs

Contraptions

Tires too thin

Dorothy

Bonk.

Dorothy concepts and layouts

antlers must follow the line

small windscreen?

mud guard

Individual windscreens
and mudguards
for rear wheel.

wheels still too little

Boot for kit

also an occasional back seat

tooght

wheels a higher

Villainy

Stankovic concepts

First Second

Published by First Second
First Second is an imprint of Roaring Brook Press, a division of
Holtzbrinck Publishing Holdings Limited Partnership
175 Fifth Avenue, New York, NY 10010

Library of Congress Control Number: 2017941166

Hardcover ISBN: 978-1-250-15984-7
Paperback ISBN: 978-1-62672-026-8

Our books may be purchased in bulk for promotional, educational, or business use.
Please contact your local bookseller or the Macmillan Corporate and Premium Sales Department
at (800) 221-7945 ext. 5442 or by e-mail at MacmillanSpecialMarkets@macmillan.com.

First edition, 2018
Book design by Taylor Esposito
Printed in China by 1010 Printing International Limited, North Point, Hong Kong

Hand drawn with Kuretake "Millenium" drawing pens on Daler Rowney
Bristol board, then scanned into Photoshop for coloring.

Hardcover: 10 9 8 7 6 5 4 3 2 1
Paperback: 10 9 8 7 6 5 4 3 2 1